123 SESAME STREET

CHRISTMAS TREASURY

RP | KIDS

PHILADELPHIA

Running Press Kids
Hachette Book Group
1290 Avenue of the Americas, New York, NY 10104
www.runningpress.com/rpkids
@RP_Kids

www.sesamestreet.org

Printed in China

First Edition: October 2018

Published by Running Press Kids, an imprint of Perseus Books, LLC, a subsidiary of Hachette Book Group, Inc. The Running Press Kids name and logo is a trademark of the Hachette Book Group.

The Hachette Speakers Bureau provides a wide range of authors for speaking events. To find out more, go to www.hachettespeakersbureau.com or call (866) 376-6591.

The publisher is not responsible for websites (or their content) that are not owned by the publisher.

Print book cover design by Frances J. Soo PIng Chow. Print book interior design by Melissa Gerber.

Library of Congress Control Number: 2017959789

ISBN: 978-0-7624-9231-2 (hardcover)

1010

10 9 8 7 6 5 4 3 2 1

TABLE OF CONTENTS

ELMO'S MERRY CHRISTMAS

It was Christmastime on Sesame Street! Everyone was excited about the holidays—especially Elmo!

A few days before Christmas, Elmo and his friends met at the community center to get ready for the big day. First, they hung pretty lights and sparkly ornaments all over the tree. Then Abby fluttered up to put the final touch on top!

Suddenly Elmo noticed that someone was missing!

"Where's Oscar?" Elmo asked. "Elmo and Elmo's friends can't celebrate without Oscar!"

"Oh, he doesn't like Christmas, Elmo," said Bert. "It makes him even more grouchy than he usually is!"

Elmo's favorite part of Christmas was making presents for his family and friends. This year, Elmo made a special gift for Oscar.

Then Elmo wrapped Oscar's present in pretty paper.
Elmo's mommy helped him tie a shiny bow around it.

The next day, everyone gathered again at the community center.

Elmo's mommy and daddy baked loads of yummy Christmas cookies. Then came the best part—decorating them!

Elmo's mommy helped everyone wrap the cookies in pretty packages to give to their friends and neighbors.

Elmo always remembered to leave a plate of cookies and a glass of milk for Santa on Christmas Eve! And Elmo didn't forget his friend Oscar!

On Christmas Eve, after a delicious dinner, Elmo and his friends and family gathered together again. This time, they walked up and down Sesame Street singing Christmas carols.

After they were finished singing, they had hot cocoa and gave each other gifts. It was a *very* merry Christmas!

Elmo loves Christmas!

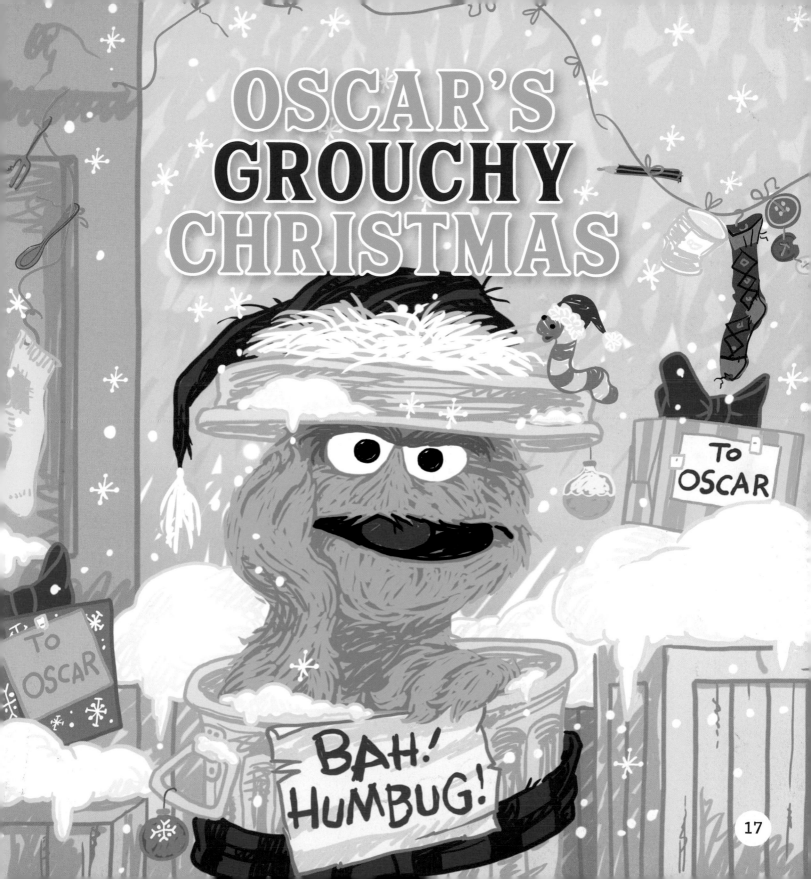

It was Christmastime on Sesame Street! Everyone was full of holiday spirit—everyone, that is, except grouchy Oscar.

Too many cheerful people were bustling around,
calling "Merry Christmas!" Oscar grumbled to himself.
This was the worst time of year for grouches!

Merry Christmas,
Oscar, old pal!

Merry Christmas?
No way!

To make matters worse, Oscar's friends tried to help him decorate his can for the holidays!

Later that day, Oscar's friends came by with Christmas presents for him, all wrapped in pretty paper. Oscar frowned. He didn't want anything new or shiny. He only wanted rotten, banged-up presents.

I, Grover, have brought this lovely gift for you, Oscar.

I hope it's an old, beat-up bicycle! If these presents are nice, I don't want them!

Later, Oscar's friends came back with some very special Christmas cookies. They knew what Oscar liked! Pickle snaps! Chocolate cookies with liver-and-pepper icing! Green gingerbread men made with spinach and brown mustard! This time, Oscar *almost* smiled. He didn't seem *quite* so grouchy. . . .

Yum! Sardine snickerdoodles! My absolute favorite!

Phew! Stinky!

On Christmas Eve, Oscar's friends showed up again. They gathered around his can and began to sing beautiful Christmas songs!

Finally, Oscar's friends returned to the community center to exchange Christmas presents. After they opened their gifts, Big Bird brought out a big garbage bag stuffed with torn wrapping paper, crushed bows, and a tangle of ribbons. He placed the bag next to Oscar's can. Everyone knew they'd found the perfect gift for their grouchy friend!

Finally, the party ended. Everyone bundled up in their warm winter clothes and headed home. Oscar was settling into his can for a long winter's nap. Snow began to fall softly onto Sesame Street. As his friends walked by his can, each one whispered, "Merry Christmas, Oscar."

A CHRISTMAS STORY

It's the night before Christmas.
What a big celebration!
Every monster is helping with
tree decoration.

BAG O'
CHRISTMAS
THINGS

Sesame Community Center

BAG O' CHRISTMAS THINGS

The stockings are hung
by the chimney with care,
in hopes jolly Santa
Claus soon will be there.

Cookie Monster is wearing a cap of bright red,
while visions of gingerbread dance in his head.

Then outside the window—do you hear that clatter?
Bert uses his flashlight to see what's the matter.

The full moon is shining on something below . . .
Super Grover has fallen—splat!—on the snow!

Then what before everyone's eyes should appear?
It's a sleigh filled with toys and eight tiny reindeer!

Sesame Community Center

The sleigh is too heavy!
Why doesn't it fly?
"The reindeer can't lift it—
and neither can I."

And then, in a twinkling, Grover has a plan.
"Teamwork's the answer. Let's all lend a hand!"

"Here, Elmo! Here, Abby!
Here, Ernie and Bert!
Go, Big Bird! Thanks, Cookie!
Everybodee, nice work!"

Sesame Community Center

Then Santa exclaims as he flies on his way,
"Merry Christmas to all! Friends helped save the day!"

CHRISTMAS SONGS FROM SESAME STREET

O Christmas Tree

O Christmas tree, O Christmas tree,
  How lovely are your branches!
O Christmas tree, O Christmas tree,
  How lovely are your branches!

Your boughs are green in summer's glow,
  And do not fade in winter's snow.
O Christmas tree, O Christmas tree,
  How lovely are your branches!

Deck the Halls

Deck the halls with boughs of holly,
  Fa-la-la-la-la, la-la-la-la.
'Tis the season to be jolly,
  Fa-la-la-la-la, la-la-la-la.
Don we now our gay apparel,
  Fa-la-la, la-la-la, la-la-la.
Troll the ancient Yuletide carol,
  Fa-la-la-la-la, la-la-la-la.

Here We Come A-Caroling

Here we come a-caroling
  Among the leaves so green.
Here we come a-wand'ring
  So fair to be seen.

Love and joy come to you,
  And to you glad tidings, too.
And God bless you and send you a
    happy New Year,
  And God send you a happy New Year.

Jingle Bells

Jingle bells, jingle bells,
  Jingle all the way!
Oh, what fun it is to ride
    In a one-horse open sleigh. Hey!

Jingle bells, jingle bells,
  Jingle all the way!
Oh, what fun it is to ride
    In a one-horse open sleigh.

BEADS

Toyland

Toyland! Toyland!
  Wonderful girl and boy land!
While you dwell within it,
  You are ever happy then.

Christmas Is Coming

Christmas is coming,
  The goose is getting fat.
Please to put a penny
  In the old man's hat.
If you haven't got a penny,
  A halfpenny will do.
If you haven't got a halfpenny,
  Then God bless you!

For Tree

Jolly Old Saint Nicholas

Jolly old Saint Nicholas,
  Lean your ear this way.
Don't you tell a single soul
  What I'm going to say.

Christmas Eve is coming soon.
  Now, you dear old man,
Whisper what you'll bring to me,
  Tell me if you can.

For Me

We Wish You a Merry Christmas

We wish you a merry Christmas,
  We wish you a merry Christmas,
We wish you a merry Christmas
  And a happy New Year.

Good tidings we bring
  To you and your kin.
Good tidings for Christmas
  And a happy New Year.

Up on the Housetop

Up on the housetop, the reindeer pause;
  Out jumps good ol' Santa Claus!
Down through the chimney with lots of toys,
  All for the little ones' Christmas joys.

Ho! Ho! Ho! Who wouldn't go?
  Ho! Ho! Ho! Who wouldn't go?
Up on the housetop, click, click, click!
  Down through the chimney with good St. Nick.

It's Christmas Again

Hang a star upon the tree,
  It's Christmas again!
Candy canes for you and me,
  It's Christmas again!

With jingle bells and pine-tree smells
  And peace on earth to men.
So wave the turkey leg on high.
  Hurrah for mince and pumpkin pie
    And Santa Claus up in the sky!
It's Christmas again!

ELMO'S DELICIOUS CHRISTMAS

It was the day before Christmas, and Elmo's kitchen smelled like sugar and cinnamon. That was because Elmo was helping his mommy and Aunt Sue bake big batches of Christmas cookies.

Elmo got to make the shapes with cookie-cutters and sprinkle on sugar that was glittery white or in bright Christmas colors.

Elmo's mommy clicked on the oven light so Elmo could watch the cookies turn golden brown. As soon as they came out of the oven, Elmo reached for some.

"Wait until they cool, and then take just one, Elmo," Mommy said. "We have to save the rest for our guests." Elmo nodded but it seemed to take forever!

"Now can Elmo pick one?" Elmo asked when the cookies were cool. "And will you tell everyone that Elmo helped make them?"

Mommy said that Elmo could tell them himself. This year he was big enough to hand out the cookies at the family's Christmas party.

Elmo smiled and picked out a cookie shaped like a reindeer.

"Mmmm . . . yummy!"

As Elmo's mommy tidied the kitchen, she glanced out the window. "Look, Elmo! It's snowing!"

"Oh, boy! Mommy, may Elmo please go outside to play?" Elmo wanted to know.

Mommy said yes, so Aunt Sue helped Elmo with his coat and boots.

"And here's a nice, warm scarf to tie around your neck," she said.

Cozy and warm, Elmo ran down Sesame Street to build a snowmonster. He saw footprints his boots made in the new snow—snow as pretty and white as the sugar Elmo had sprinkled on top of the cookies.

Snowflakes drifted down and sparkled on Elmo's hat and scarf. He opened his mouth to catch some on his tongue.

All along Sesame Street, Elmo saw his friends getting ready for the holidays. Herry was collecting toys and food for families who needed help. The Count was counting snowflakes. "One beautiful snowflake! Two beautiful snowflakes!"

"Merry Christmas, everybody!" Elmo shouted happily.

"Humph! I hate Christmas!" said Oscar, popping up from his can. "There's all that ho-ho-ho-ing and fa-la-la-ing. Everyone going around smiling and being cheerful and giving each other presents. This is the worst time of year for grouches."
Elmo couldn't believe his ears.

"Oh, Oscar!" Elmo giggled. "There are things about Christmas even a grouch would like."

"Name one," Oscar said.

Elmo thought for a moment. "Christmas cookies! Elmo helped bake some."

"Were they sardine cookies with squishy icing?" Oscar asked hopefully.

Elmo had to admit they weren't. They were oatmeal and sugar cookies. And some were shaped like candy canes and reindeer.

Oscar scowled. "Yucch! They sound awful!"

Elmo forgot all about building snowmonsters. Now he had something more important to do. "Just wait, Oscar!" Elmo said. "Elmo will be right back! Elmo is going to find a *zillion* reasons for Oscar to like Christmas!"

"Don't worry. I'm not going anywhere!" grumbled Oscar. And he disappeared inside his trash can, slamming down the lid.

Elmo set off. If he couldn't find a zillion reasons, he was sure he could find a few.

First, Elmo stopped at Big Bird's nest. Elmo told him what he wanted to do. Big Bird said, "I've got an idea! Meet me at Oscar's trash can in one hour."

Next, Elmo went to see Bert and Ernie, who were trimming their Christmas tree. They said they'd help, too.

Then Elmo visited The Count and Herry Monster. Everyone agreed to meet at Oscar's trash can.

Elmo raced home and told Aunt Sue there was something special he wanted to make. This time, *she* was the one who couldn't believe her ears.

"That sounds disgusting," Aunt Sue said doubtfully. But she helped Elmo anyway.

When everything was ready, Elmo hurried over to Oscar's. His friends
were there, just as they had promised.

"Merry Christmas, Oscar!" Elmo called as he knocked on the trash
can lid.

Oscar popped out. "I told you, I hate Christmas!"

Elmo laughed. "Not for long!"

Before Oscar could tell everyone to scram, Ernie and Bert handed him a scraggly little Christmas tree. It was decorated with a grouch in mind, with orange peels and bits of raggedy string.

"Hey, that's not a bad-looking Christmas tree," Oscar admitted.

"See, Oscar," said Elmo. "That's one thing to like about Christmas!"

"I like Christmas because it's a time for families to get together,"
said Big Bird. "Maybe Grungetta would come and visit if you invited her."
Grungetta was Oscar's best and grouchiest friend.

"Hmmm . . . ." said Oscar. "That's not the worst idea I've ever heard."

Next it was Herry's turn. "I like the holidays because they're about
helping others," he said. "Today, I collected toys and food for families who
need them. Do you have anything to share, Oscar?"

Oscar frowned. "Just a minute," he said, disappearing into his trash can.

A few seconds later he was back. "Here. Maybe somebody could use this," Oscar said, handing Herry a brand-new, red-and-white-striped scarf.

"Thanks, Oscar," said Herry. "Doesn't it feel good to help someone else?"

"Well, it sure feels good to get rid of that scarf. It doesn't have one moth hole in it," Oscar said.

Elmo saw Oscar hiding a little smile.

"Oscar, Elmo made twelve reasons for you to like Christmas!" Elmo added happily. "Here are a dozen sardine cookies with squishy icing. Merry Christmas, Oscar!"

"Ah-ah-ah!" The Count laughed. "Now, *there* is something to like about Christmas . . . your friends! Let me count them for you . . . one friend . . . two friends . . ."

"Never mind, Count! I can do it," Oscar said grouchily.

Oscar was quiet for a minute. Finally he turned to Elmo. "You were right, fuzz face. Christmas isn't so bad after all." He took a bite out of a sardine cookie. "And these cookies are disgustingly delicious. Thanks. And . . . Merry Christmas!"

Then everybody began to sing. And Oscar sang *fa-la-la* the loudest.

BIG BIRD MEETS SANTA CLAUS

It's Christmastime on Sesame Street! Today we're trimming the tree. My favorite ornament is a tiny Santa Claus with reindeer and a sleigh.

I sure would like to *meet* Santa. Wouldn't you? I wonder what Santa's doing right now.

Santa lives at the North Pole. Maybe at this very moment he's decorating *his* tree, or maybe he's hanging a Christmas wreath on his door.

If I went to the North Pole, I could meet Santa Claus. He would invite me into his house. Santa would ask me to help him get ready for Christmas.

Santa's workshop is downstairs, way below ground. There are rooms for making every different kind of toy in the world.

Santa shows me around. In the office I say, "Hello, Mrs. Claus. Pleased to meet you!" Mrs. Claus is in charge of Santa's mail. The elves use fancy computers to keep track of which child has asked for what present.

Mrs. Claus shows me the letter that I helped Elmo write! He wants a doll for Christmas. Elmo loves dolls.

Santa takes me to the workroom where the elves are making Elmo's present.

Then Santa shows me a doll that looks just like him. "Very handsome," he says. "Ho, ho, ho!"

I laugh. Santa Claus sure is a jolly old fellow.

In the next workroom, the elves are building wagons and bicycles and roller skates.

Santa asks me to be a test driver. I strap on a new pair of roller skates and I'm off! Wheeeeeee!

It's time to tidy up the wrapping room. I use a wagon to help the elves. This is the most beautiful trash I've ever seen. Oscar would be amazed!

Next I take a shiny new unicycle for a spin.
I ride through the elves' bunk room . . .

and into the reindeer stable. The reindeer give me some funny looks. They've probably never seen a bird on a unicycle before!

Now I cycle into the gym. There's Santa! He exercises every day. Santa has to keep trim so that he can slide down chimneys.

When Santa goes to change, he lets me try on his Santa costume. Look at me! I'm Santa Bird. Ho, ho, ho!

Santa takes me to the Clauses' comfy sitting room for a snack.

Mrs. Claus asks me about Sesame Street. "It's wonderful," I tell her. "I have lots of friends, and my own cozy nest, and a dog named Barkley. . . ."

Suddenly I realize that I want to go home! I don't want to miss Christmas on Sesame Street! But how am I going to get there?

It's silly of me to worry. Even though Christmas is coming and Santa is very busy, he offers to take me home to Sesame Street! I thank Santa and Mrs. Claus and say good-bye.

Then around the world Santa and I fly, through the big starry night, reindeer and sleigh and all!

And here I am, back on Sesame Street. "Ho, ho, ho!" I chuckle loudly.
"Big Bird," says Elmo, "you sound just like Santa Claus."
I chuckle even louder. Merry Christmas, everyone!

HAVE YOURSELF A FURRY LITTLE CHRISTMAS

Greetings, Elmo! I have brought the Christmas stockings for our big holiday celebration.
Oh, thank you, Grover. It's beginning to look a lot like Christmas around here.
Certainly! We shall put it all in my trusty Santa sack. Just call me Santa Grover. Off we go!

Everyone is making something for the party. Can Grover help Elmo collect everything?

We made paper garlands for the tree.
Mmm. And they soooo delicious! Want a taste?
We will save them for the tree, Cookie Monster!

We've got some silver bells . . . silver bells . . .
Jingle bells, jingle bells . . .
These will be terrific when we sing our Christmas carols.

Santa Grover is coming to town!
Ho-ho-ho to you, Santa Grover and Elmo.
When Curly wakes up, we'll bring warm apple cider for everyone.
Ooh! We're going to have a yummy time.

Does anyone know where I can find a sleigh?
You got here just in time. I just finished making presents for everyone.
Thanks, Big Bird. That's so nice of you. These snowflakes are perfect.

We have everything we need for our celebration. But Elmo thinks there's something else that's very important. What is it?
Perhaps some elves . . . *huff-huff* . . . and a few reindeer . . . *huff-puff* . . .

Now Elmo knows what Elmo was trying to remember! The most important part of Christmas is sharing it with people you love!
It *will* be a white Christmas!

WET CHRISTMAS

"I think white Christmases are yucky!
My uncle Bing Grouchby sang a hit song
years ago that describes exactly what
Christmas should be like."

I'm dreaming of a wet Christmas
Just like the ones I used to know.
When the kids stay inside,
And they can't sleigh-ride,
Because there's rain instead of snow!
   Ho, ho, ho, ho, ho, ho . . .
I'm calling for a wet Christmas
For every person that I've met.
Yes, it's puddles I'm hoping you'll get,
And may all your Christmases be wet!

A NIGHT BEFORE CHRISTMAS ON SESAME STREET

T'was the night before Christmas on Sesame Street,
And a stormy one, too, with the snow and the sleet!
All the kids in the neighborhood, snug in pajamas,
Were saying goodnight to their papas and mamas.

The house was all quiet at Ernie and Bert's
As they climbed in bed in their cozy nightshirts.
And even outside, everyone was at rest—
The Grouch in his can, the Bird in his nest.

There was one little house where not all was so comfy—
T'was the home of that famous magician named Mumfie.
He feared that the blizzard would keep Santa away,
And he thought of a bleak Christmas morn with dismay.

"This storm might be too much for Santa," he said,
"So I'll conjure some toys for the children instead."
Then he snatched up his wand, and before he could say
"A la Peanut Butter Sandwiches!" he was on his way.

A little past midnight, Ernie jumped out of bed.
He'd been jolted awake by a "thump" overhead.
As he peered at the roof, he said, "Gee, Bert, that's funny.
I thought Santa had reindeer, but that looks like a bunny!"

Ernie raced to the living room just as a foot
Had emerged from the chimney, all covered with soot.
The body that followed was equally grubby.
Said Ernie, "Why, *this* Santa's not even chubby!

"His face is all dirty, his cloak's black as night.
But I *always* thought Santa wore red and white!
He has only a stick poking out of his pouch,
And these gifts should have gone to Oscar the Grouch!"

Ernie hopped back in bed and was soon sound asleep,
But poor Mumford had other appointments to keep.
With his team of white rabbits, the brave little wizard
Continued his trip through the terrible blizzard.

Mumfie's magic did wonders on that Christmas Eve,
But the gifts he created were hard to believe!
There was seed for a bird by the Count's Christmas tree,
And the sneakers for Big Bird were only size three!

Little Grover had hoped for a new teddy bear,
But his gift was a ribbon for Betty Lou's hair.
And if you think that Grover was pretty unlucky,
Bert's soap dish was intended for poor Rubber Duckie.

As the morning came, Mumford drove home through the drifts.
He had made all his rounds, given everyone gifts.
So imagine his shock when he walked in to see
A fat, jolly old man sitting there by his tree!

"Mumford, my friend," Santa said with a smile,
"I've been two steps behind you for quite a long while.
Though you've made some unusual gift selections,
You've done a fine job, with my little corrections.

"I followed your sleigh and erased all your traces.
You left all the right gifts, but in all the wrong places!
I just made a few switches so no one would know
That old Santa Claus was held up by the snow.

"But the meaning of Christmas is not gifts, my boy;
It's the impulse to do things that bring others joy.
Though your magical wand can't do everything right,
The true magic of Christmas was with you tonight!"

With a nod of his head and wink of his eye,
Santa hopped in his sleigh and took off for the sky.
He was heard to exclaim as he flew out of sight,
"A LA PEANUT BUTTER SANDWICHES!
AND TO ALL A GOOD NIGHT!"

OSCAR'S CHRISTMAS CAROL

"Bah, Humbug!" Oscar said loudly just as Big Bird and Betty Lou walked by. "Bah, humbug!" he said again as they stopped to stare.

"Whatever that means, it sure sounds grouchy," said Betty Lou. "What's the matter, Oscar?"

"Nothing's the matter," Oscar answered. "Everything's great. I'm reading a terrific story about a mean old fellow named Mr. Scrooge. He hated Christmas, so he said, 'Bah, humbug!' all the time. He sounds like my uncle Smarmy. He might even be a relative of mine!"

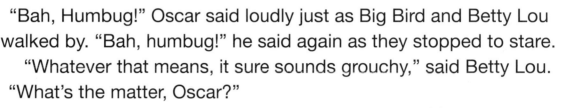

"How could anyone hate Christmas?" asked Betty Lou. "Everyone is good and kind at Christmas, and there are good things to eat, and songs to sing and presents to give. Christmas is a happy time, Oscar."

"Bah, humbug!" Oscar replied. "Mr. Scrooge had a way of fixing that. Not only was he miserable himself, but he ruined everyone else's Christmas, too. He even made his helper, Bob Cratchit, work on Christmas Eve! Boy, that's a real grouch for you!"

"Hey, wait a minute," said Big Bird. "I know that story. It's 'A Christmas Carol,' by Mr. Charles Dickens. Maria read it to me last Christmas. And guess what, Oscar. It has a happy ending!"

"How could it?" asked Oscar in disgust. "This guy Scrooge was such a great grouch! He's my hero—an inspiration! I want to be just like him."

"Well, then," said Big Bird, "you'll have to stop being a grouch, because that's what Scrooge did. He had a dream that showed him how wrong he had been about Christmas. You should read the rest of the book, Oscar."

"Bah, humbug," said Oscar as he disappeared into his can.

A little later, Big Bird passed Oscar's can again on his way home from Betty Lou's house. "Merry Christmas, Bird!" shouted Oscar as he popped out.

Big Bird looked at Oscar in surprise. "Why, Oscar, you changed your mind. You must have had a dream, just like Mr. Scrooge did, and now you're not going to be a grouch any more!"

"Ho, ho, ho, no, no, no!" said Oscar. "That's not what happened. I was giving that dumb book with the happy ending to the trash man just after you left, and he reminded me that Christmas is a holiday. You know what that means, Bird?"

"Sure," said Big Bird. "A holiday is a day when everyone is good and kind and celebrates . . ."

"No, no," broke in Oscar. "It means that there's no trash pick-up that day, and I get to keep my wonderful trash one more day! What a gift! Merry Christmas, Bird!"

A CHRISTMAS POEM BY BIG BIRD

Everyone seems to think that
Christmas comes just once a year,
On December twenty-fifth. Or so they say.
But I remember other times
That were really very special,
And I know they didn't come on Christmas Day!

In the spring I had the sniffles
And was feeling simply awful,
And I didn't know exactly what to do.
Mr. Hooper brought me chicken soup,
And soon I was all better.
And you know, that really seemed
Like Christmas too!

At our street bazaar last summer
Betty Lou won all the pies.
Now, I must admit, that seemed a bit unfair.
But when she cut them into pieces,
And she gave us each a slice,
Did you notice there was Christmas in the air?

In the fall, when Herry's kitten
Climbed a tree and she got stuck,
I knew that I would have to do my part.
So I stretched myself real tall
And I gave a helping hand,
With a Christmas kind of feeling in my heart.

I am sure it doesn't matter
If it rains or if it snows.
Christmas doesn't seem to care about the weather.
Being good to one another
Summer, winter, fall and spring
Makes it Christmastime whenever we're together.

137

JOLLY OLD ST. NICHOLAS

Jolly old Saint Nicholas,
Lean your ear this way.
Don't you tell a single soul
What I'm going to say.
Christmas Eve is coming soon.
Now, you dear old man,
Whisper what you'll bring to me.
Tell me if you can.

When the clock is striking twelve,
When we're fast asleep,
Down the chimney broad and black
With your pack you'll creep.
All the stockings you will find,
Hanging in neat rows.
Mine's the one you'll notice first,
'Cause it has three toes!

Ernie wants a little friend
For his Rubber Duckie.
Oscar wants a worn-out shoe.
He thinks toys are yucchy!
Bert would like some bottle caps,
But for me, Saint Nick,
I'd prefer to be surprised,
So I'll let *you* pick!

THOUGHTS THAT COUNT

Dear Mommy,
How can I help you?
Let me count the ways!
I can keep my bedroom tidy,
And be good on rainy days.
I am sure to be a little help
In everything you do.
Why, there must be a million ways
To show that I love you!

Here is a way to give your best gift—yourself!
Give gift cards that make promises you can keep!

Rosie

BIRD SEED

141

A WRAP SESSION

Early on Christmas Eve, everyone gathered to wrap presents before the big Christmas party. But nobody had remembered to bring any wrapping paper or ribbons! Just then, Oscar the Grouch arrived with his gifts all wrapped up in newspaper and tied with bits of old string.

"Hey, Oscar, what a good idea!" said Betty Lou. "We don't need fancy paper and ribbons. We can wrap our presents with all kinds of things we find around the house!"

Just as they were finishing wrapping the gifts, Prairie Dawn looked out the window. "Oh, look!" she cried. "It's snowing! It's going to be a white Christmas after all! Let's go caroling."

And that's just what they did.

WE WISH YOU A MERRY CHRISTMAS

We wish you a merry Christmas
We wish you a merry Christmas
We wish you a merry Christmas
And a happy New Year!

We all want some Figgy Fizz punch
We all want some Figgy Fizz punch
We all want some Figgy Fizz punch
So bring it right here!

We won't go until we get some
We won't go until we get some
We won't go until we get some
It's a cup of good cheer!

BERT'S AUNT WILLY'S CRISPY OATMEAL COOKIES

1 stick of butter   ⅓ cup of sugar   2¼ cups of oats

Let the butter soften at room temperature so you can work it with your hands. Put all the ingredients into a mixing bowl and knead them until they're well blended. Roll the dough into walnut-size balls. On a board, flatten the balls with the back of a fork until they are very thin. Use a spatula to transfer the cookies to an ungreased baking sheet. Ask a grown-up to bake them for about eight minutes, or until golden brown, in a 325° oven.

BERT'S FIGGY FIZZ PUNCH (SERVES 4)

One 11-ounce jar of whole figs in syrup, chilled
20-ounce root beer

Put a whole fig and one tablespoon of syrup into four glasses. Fill up each glass with root beer and stir. Serve Figgy Fizz Punch with long spoons so everyone can eat the fig in the bottom of each glass.

WHITE CHRISTMAS

I dreamed of snow for Christmas.
There were visions in my head
Of a snowball fight, a snowman,
And me riding on my sled.

If there isn't snow for Christmas,
I will simply have to fake it.
If I can't go out and play in it,
I'll just stay home and make it!

ELMO'S CHRISTMAS STORY

Christmas is almost here! Everyone on Sesame Street is in the Christmas spirit. Murray helps his neighbors choose the perfect Christmas tree to decorate. Big Bird and Abby spin and zip around on ice skates. Elmo, Zoe, Rosita, and Prairie Dawn have lots of fun in the snow. Who looks like Santa Claus?

SAFE
SKA

TREES

Elmo thinks school is even MORE fun during the winter holidays. *Snip! Snip!* Rosita makes paper snowflakes. *Squirt! Squirt!* Zoe uses sweet icing on her gingerbread house. *Nom nom, crunch, crunch!* Cookie Monster, you should wait until after Christmas to eat your gingerbread house!

SCRAM

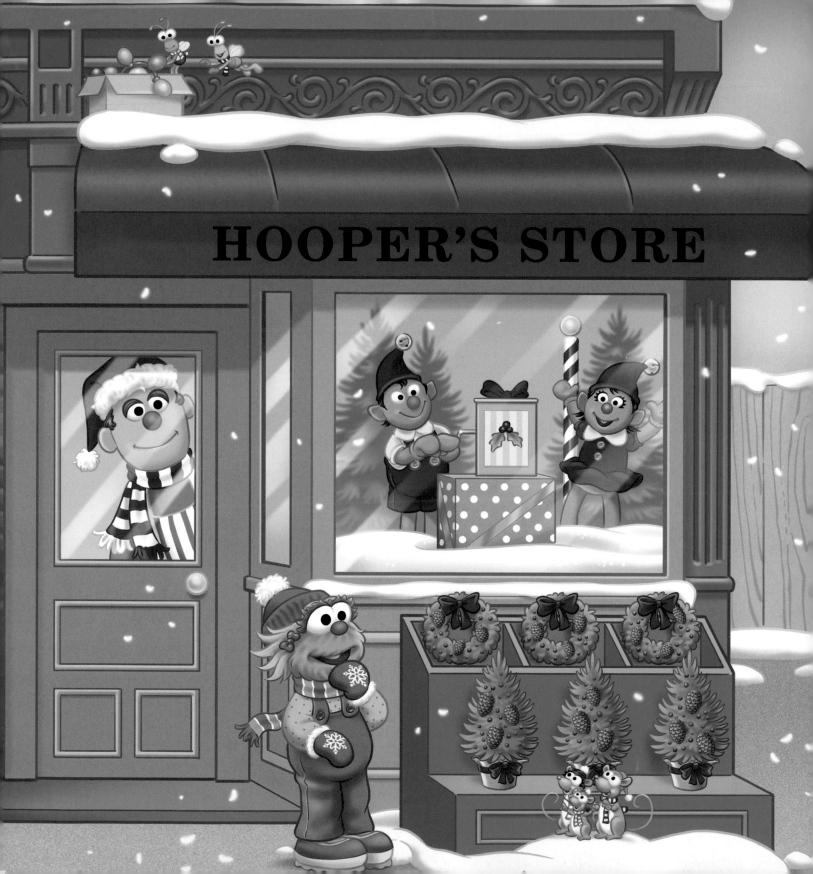

Jingle bells! Jingle bells! Jingle all the way! Elmo likes to sing carols in the neighborhood at Christmastime. It's a good way to spend time with friends. Right, Oscar?

Elmo thinks the best part of Christmas is counting down the days until Santa comes! Merry Christmas!

TAXI

1234

FRIENDLY FROSTY MONSTERS

"Yay! Yippee! It's a monstrously snowy day on Sesame Street!"

Zip and clip!

On with snowsuits and rubber boots. Sometimes you need a big brother—or Big Bird—to help.

wigg

Clasp and snap!

, waggle!

Tussle, tug!

Slippery-slide on skiddy skates.
Watch out or you'll wobble!

"Oh, dear! Oh, no!" weeps Little Bo-Peep.
"My woolly white sheep ran away in the snow!
Where did they go?"

Run and romp!

Baaaa

Slide
and
stomp!

Can you help find all ten?
Plus one shivery black sheep!

Baby Bear slides happily down the hill!
Jack and Jill come tumbling after.

Whish, swish, vroom!

"Ah! I love to count fluffy flakes!
One wonderful flake!
Two terrific flakes!
Three thrilling flakes!
Four fabulous flakes . . ."

In a wintry wood, Red Riding Hood
enjoys a walk with Bert.
(But beware of that watchful wolf!)

Making friendly, frosty monsters is easy
if you try. Big button eyes—with a snazzy
schnoz or a frosty frown.

Pat! Pack!

Roll it 'round!

Grouches and monsters like a good, old-fashioned snowball fight!

Chuck

Huff, puff!

Off with boots, hats,
and monster mittens.
Inside for songs—
and milk for the
three little kittens.

Sip
Sip
Slurp

Mmm! Creamy, steamy cocoa!

Then it's time to head home to curl up under a warm, comfy blanket.

Blue blankies and pink pillows for little Twiddles.

Now only moonlight plays
on the snow.

Night-night,
Elmo!

Snoozzzzzzz...

I CAN'T WAIT UNTIL CHRISTMAS

"How long is it until Christmas, Granny?" Big Bird asked.
They had just finished a Thanksgiving dinner of corn-kernel salad, birdseed roast with sesame-seed gravy, and pumpkin-seed pie.

"Only four weeks," Granny told him.

"Four whole weeks!" Big Bird said. "I can't wait!"

"Christmas will be here before you know it," said Granny. "What do you want for Christmas?"

"A new baseball bat, please," Big Bird said. "What do you want?"

"I would like a surprise," she said. "I still remember the nicest Christmas surprise I ever had. One Christmas, when I was a little chick, my grandpa made me a birdhouse.

"It had a pointed green-shingled roof, red sides with little windows, a round doorway, a birdseed box, and a perch in the front where the birds could rest or sing a song. Every time a bird perched on it, I thought of Grandpa."

"May I see it?" Big Bird asked.

"I'm afraid not," she said sadly. "It got broken a long time ago."

Now Big Bird knew what to give Granny for Christmas.

When Big Bird got back to Sesame Street, he asked Maria to help him make his surprise for Granny. "It has to look just like this," he told her, showing her the picture he had drawn.

Big Bird and Maria cut out pieces of wood and hammered them together. They glued the shingles on the roof, painted the sides, and drew little windows on them. Finally they attached a birdseed box and nailed a perch onto the front.

"Do you think Granny will like it?" Big Bird asked Maria.

"It's beautiful, Big Bird," Maria told him. "And it's a wonderful present because you made it for her."

"I'll send it to her right away!" Big Bird said. "I can't wait for Granny to see it!"

"You'll ruin the surprise," said Maria. "Wrap it up and give it to her for Christmas."

Big Bird wrapped the birdhouse in some sparkly Christmas paper. Then he called Granny on the phone.

"How long is it until Christmas, Granny?" he asked her.

"Three whole weeks?" said Big Bird. "I can't wait!"

"I already have your surprise present," he told Granny. "Do you want me to tell you what it is?"

"No," Granny said. "I want it to be a surprise. Why don't you make your Christmas cards and visit Santa Claus. Then it won't seem so long until Christmas."

Big Bird made cards for everyone on Sesame Street and delivered them to all his friends. Then he and Snuffy went to Nickles Department Store and waited in line to see Santa.

Snuffy sat on Santa's lap first. "I want a skateboard for me and a baseball bat for my friend Big Bird," he said.

"Ho, ho, ho!" Santa laughed. "That will have to be a very big skateboard!"
Then it was Big Bird's turn. "I want a baseball bat and a visit from
Granny," he said. "And please remember a skateboard for my friend Snuffy."
"Ho, ho, ho!" Santa said.

"How long is it until Christmas?" Big Bird asked Granny on the phone.

"Two whole weeks? I can't wait! I've delivered all my cards, I've seen Santa, and I already have your present. Do you want me to tell you what it is?"

"No," Granny said. "I want it to be a surprise. Why don't you get a Christmas tree to decorate. Then it won't seem so long until Christmas."

So Big Bird and his friends went to pick out a tree for Big Bird. Bert picked a tall, skinny tree. Ernie liked a short, fat one. Oscar wanted a scruffy tree with hardly any needles. And the Count spent so much time counting trees, he couldn't choose one at all.

Back at Big Bird's nest, everyone helped him decorate his tree. Oscar tied on old shoes and hubcaps. Bert draped a shiny garland of paper clips. Ernie strung popcorn, and the Count added bat decorations.

Big Bird made paper rings and a tinfoil star.
Even Oscar agreed it was a wonderful Christmas
tree. "Especially the part with the trash," he said.

"How long is it until Christmas?" Big Bird asked Granny again.

"A whole week? I can't wait! I decorated my Christmas tree, and I already have your surprise present. Do you want me to give you one teeny, tiny hint?"

"No," Granny said. "I want it to be a surprise. Why don't you make Christmas cookies. Then the week won't seem so long."

So Cookie Monster and Big Bird made Christmas cookies. Big Bird saved some cookies to eat with Granny. But Cookie Monster gobbled his right up.

"You've eaten all your cookies!" Big Bird said.

"No problem." Cookie Monster patted his tummy and smiled. "Me make more cookies every day until Christmas."

Finally, on the day before Christmas, Granny arrived. Big Bird ran to greet her.

"How long is it until Christmas, Granny?" Big Bird asked.

"Only one more day," she answered.

"One whole day? I can't wait!" Big Bird said.

Granny gave Big Bird a long, skinny present. "Merry Christmas," she said.

"Is it a ski pole? A golf club? An umbrella?" Big Bird guessed.

"You'll just have to wait until tomorrow, Big Bird," said Granny.

Then Big Bird gave Granny the wrapped birdhouse. "Merry Christmas," he said.

"I wonder what it could be," she said. "A pocketbook? A bread box? A new hat?"

Big Bird laughed. "It would make a silly hat. Do you want a little hint?"

"No," Granny said. She put her gift under the tree. "I want it to be a surprise."

Granny and Big Bird hung their stockings. They put out a plate of cookies and a glass of milk for Santa.

Big Bird looked at Granny's present under the tree. "Are you sure you don't want one teeny, tiny, itty-bitty, little hint?" he asked Granny. "You'll never be able to guess what it is."

"No," Granny told him. "I want it to be a surprise. Go to sleep, Big Bird, and Christmas will be here in the morning."

"I can't wait!" Big Bird said and yawned. "I'll never be able to sleep. I won't even be able to close my . . ."

The next thing Big Bird knew, it was morning—Christmas morning at last! The first thing he did was give Granny her present.

"What a wonderful surprise!" Granny said happily. "It's just like the one Grandpa Bird made me!" She hugged Big Bird. "And it's special because you made it for me. Every time a bird perches on it and sings me a song, I'll think of you."

Big Bird tore the ribbons and wrapping off the gift Granny brought him. "A baseball bat! It's just what I wanted," he said. "Thank you, Granny."

Big Bird took a couple of practice swings with his new bat. "This has been the best Christmas ever."

"Next year we can do it all over again," said Granny.

"Next year? A whole year until Christmas!" said Big Bird. "I can't wait!"

ELMO'S CHRISTMAS COLORS

Deck the halls with red and green
and pink and gold and blue!
Elmo loves all Christmas colors—
do you like them, too?

Red striped candy canes . . .

blue paper chains.

Gold sparkly bows . . .

when it snows!

Orange toys
for juggling . . .

a pink quilt for snuggling.

Shiny yellow skis . . .

green Christmas trees.

Purple pies baking . . .

silver bells shaking.

Now our colors are all done—
Merry Christmas, everyone!

ELMO'S A–MAZE–ING CHRISTMAS

Come along to Sesame's Christmas celebration!
Where should Abby and friends hang each decoration?
Hint: On something TALL and GREEN.

Big Bird has a very puzzled look on his face.
He wonders: "What is missing on this fireplace?"
Hint: It's something SOFT that could fit on a FOOT.

Cookie Monster would like something tasty to eat.
Will you help him find his all-time favorite Christmas treat?
Hint: It's something ROUND and SWEET and YUMMY.

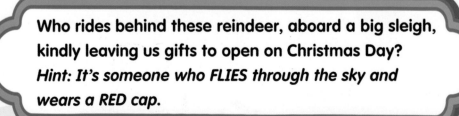

Who rides behind these reindeer, aboard a big sleigh, kindly leaving us gifts to open on Christmas Day?
Hint: It's someone who FLIES through the sky and wears a RED cap.

What shines and sparkles so brightly up above, as a sign of Christmas joy and peace and love?

Hint: It's something POINTY that GLOWS.

ELMO'S CHRISTMAS SNOWMAN

It was the day before Christmas on Sesame Street. Elmo and his friends had been wishing for a white Christmas.

"Look, Abby," Elmo said happily. "It's snowing! Now Elmo and Abby can make a snowman!"

Abby wasn't so sure. It was hardly snowing and the ground wasn't white at all.

"We need a lot of snow, Elmo," she said. "We have to make three big balls."

"What if everyone collects snow from all over the neighborhood? Maybe that would be enough," Elmo said. So Abby and Elmo went to find their friends.

The snow began to fall a little faster. Now Sesame Street was beginning to look a little more Christmasy. But there still didn't seem to be enough snow for a big, fat snowman.

Big Bird scraped together snow from a couple of windowsills.
Zoe collected some from the tops of mailboxes.
"I cleared snow from all the benches in the park," said Bert.

But there *still* wasn't enough to make three big, round balls for a snowman.

Elmo rolled a tiny snowball along the ground, going round and round as he tried to get enough snow for the third ball.

"This is all there is for the snowman's head," Elmo said sadly.

"Brrr. I'm getting cold," Abby said with a little shiver.

"And it's almost time for Santa to come, everybodeee," Grover added.

Elmo added his little ball to the top of the snowman.
"We'll make a bigger snowman tomorrow," Zoe said
when she saw Elmo's disappointment.
"I *like* our little snowman!" said Abby.
"We had fun!" Big Bird added.

Suddenly Ernie began to laugh.
"Hey, look at Elmo!" he called. "He looks just like . . ."
". . . a SNOWMAN!" everyone yelled. "ELMO is Elmo's Christmas snowman! Now it really does feel like Christmas!"

ELMO'S CHRISTMAS PICTURE PUZZLES AND SONGS

Spot these things in the snow.

Jingle Bells

Jingle bells, jingle bells,
Jingle all the way!
Oh, what fun it is to ride
In a one-horse open sleigh. Hey!

254

Now search for five differences
between the two pictures.
For the solution, turn to page 266.

Jingle bells, jingle bells,
Jingle all the way!
Oh, what fun it is to ride
In a one-horse open sleigh. Hey!

Search for these wintry items near the ice.

Here We Come A-Caroling

Here we come a-caroling
Among the leaves so green.
Here we come a-wandering
So fair to be seen.

Now find five things that are different
in the two ice-skating pictures.
For the solution, turn to page 266.

SAFE TO
SKATE

Love and joy come to you,
 And to you glad tidings, too.
And God bless you and send you
 A happy New Year,
And God send you a happy New Year.

257

Find these holiday things around the tree.

O Christmas Tree

O Christmas tree, O Christmas tree,
How lovely are your branches!
O Christmas tree, O Christmas tree,
How lovely are your branches!

Now look for five things that are
different in the two pictures.
For the solution, turn to page 267.

Your boughs are green in summer's glow,
And do not fade in winter's snow.
O Christmas tree, O Christmas tree,
How lovely are your branches!

Deck the Halls

Deck the halls with boughs of holly,
Fa-la-la-la-la, la-la-la-la.
'Tis the season to be jolly,
Fa-la-la-la-la, la-la-la-la.

Now search for five differences
in the two pictures.
For the solution, turn to page 267.

Don we now our gay apparel,
Fa-la-la, la-la-la, la-la-la.
Troll the ancient yuletide carol,
Fa-la-la-la-la, la-la-la-la.

261

Search for these holiday things in the store.

Up on the Housetop

Up on the housetop reindeer pause,
Out jumps good old Santa Claus!
Down through the chimney with lots of toys,
All for the little ones' Christmas joys.

Now find five differences between
the two pictures.
For the solution, turn to page 268.

Ho ho ho! Who wouldn't go?
Ho ho ho! Who wouldn't go?
Up on the housetop, click, click, click!
Down through the chimney with good St. Nick.

Find these things at the holiday celebration.

We Wish You a Merry Christmas

We wish you a merry Christmas,
We wish you a merry Christmas,
We wish you a merry Christmas,
And a happy New Year!

Now find five differences between the two pictures.
For the solution, turn to page 268.

Good tidings we bring
To you and your kin,
Good tidings for Christmas,
And a happy New Year!

This is the answer key to the Picture Puzzle on pages 254 & 255.

This is the answer key to the Picture Puzzle on pages 256 & 257.

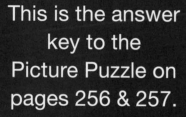

This is the answer key to the Picture Puzzle on pages 258 & 259.

This is the answer key to the Picture Puzzle on pages 260 & 261.

This is the answer key to the Picture Puzzle on pages 262 & 263.

This is the answer key to the Picture Puzzle on pages 264 & 265.

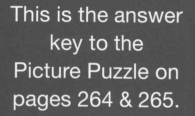

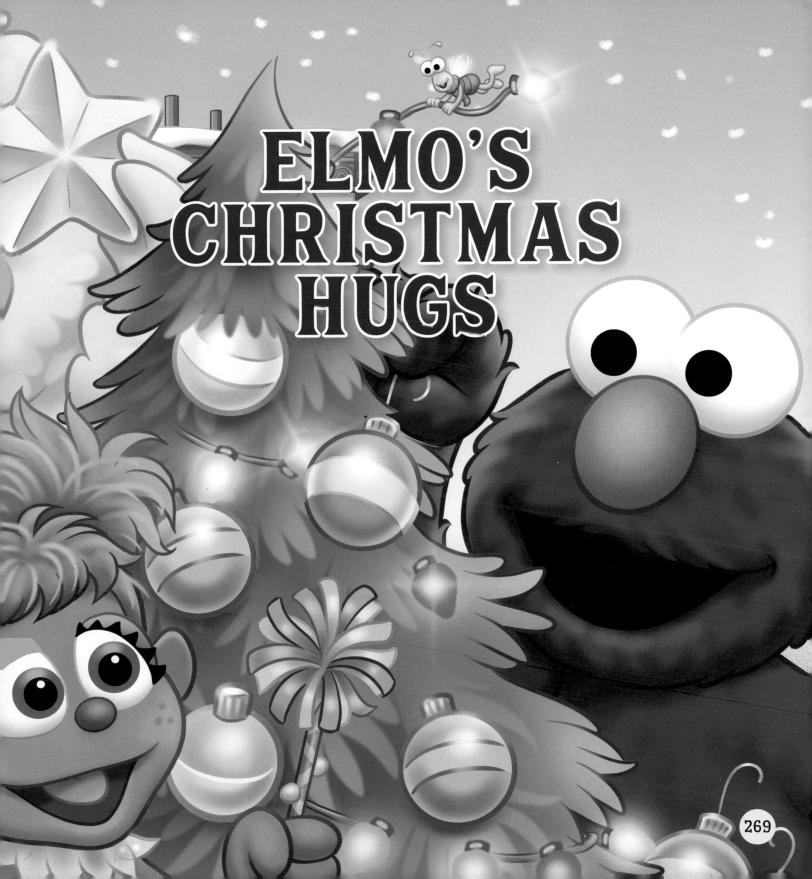

ELMO'S CHRISTMAS HUGS

Christmas isn't far away
when winter days grow snowy,
and when Elmo builds snowmonsters
with advice and laughs from Zoe!

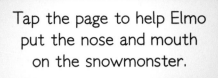
Tap the page to help Elmo put the nose and mouth on the snowmonster.

Elmo goes to Grandma's house
to help bake Christmas sweets.
He loves just being with her—
even more than all the treats!

COOKIES

How would you
decorate the
gingerbread house?

Elmo always joins with friends
to trim a Christmas tree.
The twinkling lights and tinsel
are so magical to see!

Elmo lends a hand to help
wrap packages each year
to give to those who need a smile,
some kindness, hope, and cheer.

Help Elmo choose a
special bow for the present.

Carols come with Christmas
just like wreaths and mistletoe;
Elmo always sings up high
while Cookie sings down low!

More than gifts and songs and sweets,
and more than snowy weather,
what Elmo loves are Christmas hugs
that bring everyone together!

Give yourself
a big holiday hug!

TO: ERNIE
FROM: BERT

"My bottle cap collection always brings back fond memories. This cap is from a Figgy Fizz I drank last Arbor Day in the park. And this cap is from the bottle I used to make some frozen Figgy Pops just last Tuesday. Now I need to use these bottle caps to make Ernie's Christmas present. Oh, well. I still have my oatmeal box collection."

Here's what you need to make picture ornaments:

a bunch of bottle caps
some pictures from magazines or old Christmas cards
glue
yarn

Here's what you do:
1. Cut out some beautiful little pictures
   in circles just big enough to fit inside
   a bottle cap.
2. Glue the pictures inside the bottle caps with a dab of glue.
3. Put another dab of glue on the back of the bottle cap and stick
   on a long piece of yarn.
4. Tie the yarn in a loop with a pretty bow.
5. Hang these cute little framed pictures on your Christmas tree.
   After Christmas, you can hang them in your room—from a bedpost,
   a doorknob, a picture hook, or anywhere!

THE COUNT'S 12 DAYS OF CHRISTMAS CALENDAR

Do you know the song, "The Twelve Days of Christmas"?
This is The Count's own version.

On the *first* day of Christmas
My good friends gave to me
One new bat for my belfry.

On the *second* day of Christmas
My good friends gave to me
Two spiffy spats.

One the *third* day of Christmas
My good friends gave to me
Three silk scarves.

On the *fourth* day of Christmas
My good friends gave to me
Four cozy capes.

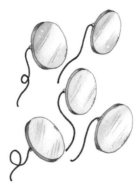

On the *fifth* day of Christmas
My good friends gave to me
Five magnificent monocles.

On the *sixth* day of Christmas
My good friends gave to me
Six pairs of pants.

On the *seventh* day of Christmas
My good friends gave to me
Seven jersey jackets.

On the *eighth* day of Christmas
My good friends gave to me
Eight nifty neckties.

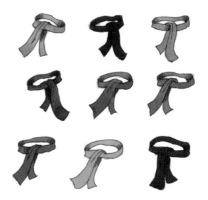

On the *ninth* day of Christmas
My good friends gave to me
Nine silly sashes.

On the *tenth* day of Christmas
My good friends gave to me
Ten grand gloves.

On the *eleventh* day of Christmas
My good friends gave to me
Eleven knitted knee socks.

One the *twelfth* day of Christmas
My good friends gave to me
Twelve great galoshes.

NUTCRACKER SWEETS

"Oh, my goodness, Herry. What a lot of nuts you have here. It must have taken a very long time to get them all out of their cute little shells."

"I cracked nuts all day long to make my favorite Christmas treats for the Christmas Eve party. Ya!"

Candied Nuts

Here's what you need to make candied nuts:

½ cup brown sugar, packed firm
¼ cup granulated sugar
⅓ cup half-and-half milk and cream
½ teaspoon almond extract
1½ cups whole almonds
a candy thermometer
a grown-up to help you

Here's what you do:

Put all the sugar and the half-and-half into a saucepan and stir over low heat until the sugar is dissolved. Continue to cook over low heat, without stirring, until the temperature, measured on a candy thermometer, reaches 240 degrees. The mixture will be syrupy, and will form a soft ball when a little bit is dropped into cold water.

Add the almond extract and the almonds, and stir the nuts until they are coated with syrup. Spoon them out onto wax paper or foil, and separate them with a fork. As they cool, the coating will harden.

You will have two cups of candied nuts.

"You must be very handy with a nutcracker, Herry."

"What's a nutcracker?"

Spiced Nuts:

Here's what you need to make spiced nuts:

1 tablespoon egg white
2 cups pecans or walnuts
⅓ cup sugar
1 teaspoon cinnamon
¼ teaspoon nutmeg

Here's what you do:

Put the nuts into a mixing bowl and add the egg white. Stir until all the nuts are sticky

Mix the sugar and spices. Sprinkle the mixture on the nuts and stir until the nuts are coated with it. Spread the nuts on an ungreased baking sheet and ask a grown-up to bake them in a 300° oven for 30 minutes. Makes two cups of spiced nuts.

COOKIE MONSTER'S CHRISTMAS TREE

"Me in big trouble, Betty Lou! Me want to hang pretty cookies on tree,
but cookies always look good enough to eat."

"I'll help you make some cookies that even you won't eat, Cookie Monster. Then you can
put them on your tree instead."

Here's what you need to make "cookie" ornaments:

1 can of children's white or yellow air-drying modeling compound	*watercolor paints*
ribbon or yarn	*breadboard and small rolling pin*
a pencil	*clear shellac*

Here's what you do:
1. Roll out a chunk of the modeling dough with the rolling pin until it is about $\frac{1}{8}$ of an inch thick.
2. Cut out cookie shapes, using either cookie cutters or a drinking glass.
3. Punch a hole with the pencil about ¼ inch from the top of the "cookie" shape.
4. Let the "cookies" dry overnight and then decorate them with watercolor paints.
5. After the paint has dried, cover the "cookies" with shellac if you want them to last.
6. Thread the ribbon or yarn through the holes, tie some nice bows, and hang these "cookie" ornaments on your tree.

Note: To make your own modeling dough, take one slice of stale white bread with crusts and one-half teaspoon of white glue for each "cookie". Knead chunks of bread with glue until the mixture feels like dough. Children can shape and flatten "cookies" with their hands. Then follow steps 3 to 6.

288

ELMO'S NIGHT BEFORE CHRISTMAS

'Twas the night before Christmas, all quiet and bright,
and Sesame Street slept under a blanket of white.
The Honkers were silent, and made nary a peep.
The Grouches had tucked in for their grouchy Christmas sleep.
Ernie in his stockings and Bert in his cap
had just settled down for their Christmas Eve nap.
Every monster lay sleeping in this quiet neighborhood,
but one who wanted to stay up if he could.

SCRAM!

That monster was Elmo, with fur fuzzy and red.
He just had to meet Santa! He couldn't go to bed!
As Elmo grew sleepy waiting next to his tree,
he heard a loud noise that filled him with glee.

Thank You,
Santa.
Love, Elmo

It came from above, that noise like a CLANG.
Santa's up on the roof—Elmo knew from the BANG.
He rushed to the window. Had Santa come?
But nothing was there. "What was that noise from?"
Elmo wondered out loud, as he scratched his sleepy head.
"Is Santa up there? Elmo heard his big sled!"

With some footsteps behind him, Elmo turned right around
and saw Santa slide down the chimney with almost no sound!
"Ho, ho, ho!" Santa said. "I made scarcely a peep!
How is it I woke you—weren't you asleep?
Now come, little monster, and sit on my knee—
and tell me, did you stay up waiting for me?"

Thank You,
Santa.
Love, Elmo

"Elmo wants to be honest and won't tell a lie.
Elmo did stay up late, but there's a reason why.
Elmo thinks there is something that you need to hear.
Everyone really loves your good holiday cheer.
Elmo knows that your job is a big one to do—
Elmo just wants to give his thanks to you.
And one more thing Elmo wants to say,
your suit and my fur are matching today!"

And just like that, Santa started to giggle.
And when Santa giggled, his whole body jiggled.
"Elmo," said Santa, "what a nice thing to say!
When you tell someone, 'thank you,'
    it can make his whole day.
Now run along to your bedroom and go get some rest.
You've helped make this Christmas one of my best."

Back in his bedroom, Elmo lay in his bed,
while outside the window, Santa flew by in his sled.
Elmo heard Santa say, as he flew out of sight,
"Merry Christmas to all, and to Elmo, good night!"

THE END

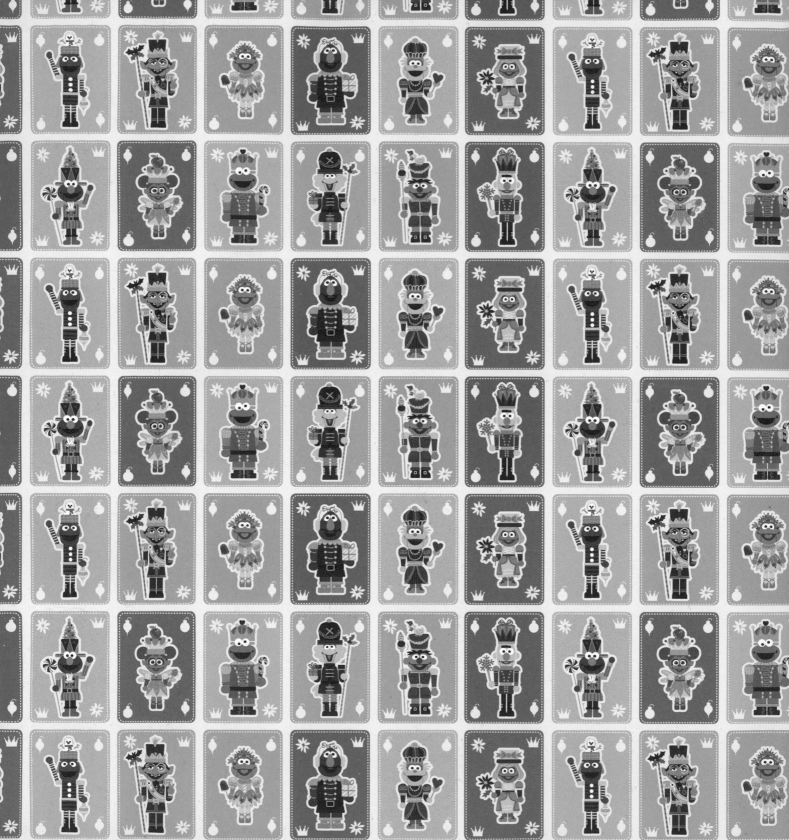